MY ADVENTURE WITH YOU

THE SUMMER UNPLUGGED EPILOGUES BOOK 3

AMY SPARLING

AMY SPARLING

ONE
KEANNA

I HAVEN'T BEEN this nervous in a long time. Maybe I've *never* been this nervous. Some events in my life have been nerve-wracking in a terrifying way, like how I lived a broken, sad life with my birth mother before I found a better home, or nerve-wracking in a surprising way, like when my friends surprised me with a perfect small, intimate surprise wedding. Right now, I'm feeling nervous... in a complicated way.

Because I just graduated college.

I got my diploma—well, the fake diploma they hand you on stage because the official one gets mailed to you—and I didn't trip and fall, and I'm pretty sure I smiled and didn't blink when the camera flash went off to take my photo before I stepped off the stage. And then I made it all the way back to my chair in this massive stadium filled with graduates while the roar of cheering and clapping filled the air, and I didn't puke. All in all, it's been a successful graduation.

Getting my associate degree a few years ago was an accomplishment that felt amazing, but this is even better. Now I have a bachelor's degree in business management. It took so much longer than I'd planned. But I guess that's what happens sometimes. We can plan for things to go smoothly, but they hardly ever do. It took me nearly four years after getting my associate degree to finish this one. What was supposed to be two years of full-time course work turned into four years of part time course work, a few re-taken classes, dropped classes, and lots of stress. College is hard. It's even harder when you're working full time.

I love my job at The Track, especially because my bosses are my parents and in-laws, so it doesn't get much more fun than that, but fun bosses didn't make college any easier. I wasn't exactly the greatest student when I was in grade school. It also kind of sucked that I was older than most other people in my classes. I'm twenty-five now, and half of the people who are graduating with me today are twenty-two, and single, and living crazy lives in dorm rooms, drinking and partying every night. I live with my husband in our own house. I feel like an old grandma in comparison to my classmates.

Oh well, it's all over now. I have my degree, and I've accomplished the one thing I've always wanted to do. Now I get to celebrate.

After the graduation ceremony—which takes forever, by the way—I wander outside of the stadium to find my family. There are hundreds of people here, graduates in long black graduation gowns, and families, smiling and taking pictures. I'd told Jett I'd find him near the B entrance, but once I walk around to that side of the stadium, it's filled with so many people who must have all had the same idea.

I chew on the inside of my lip, scanning the crowds of people, hoping to find the people who belong to me. All around me, graduates are posing with their family, smiling for pictures. A confetti popper goes off beside me, coating the air with colorful bits of paper while someone squeals their delight at graduating.

I wander around some more, wondering where

the heck everyone went. I know they're here. They have to be. Jett and I drove here together, but the rest of my family was supposed to come watch me graduate.

"Key!"

The child-like shout sounds just like my seven-year-old little brother, Elijah. I whip my head around, looking for his reddish-brown hair, finally finding him a dozen feet away. He's wearing the cutest little khaki dress pants, shiny black shoes, and a red button up shirt that matches my university colors. He waves at me as I walk over, finally finding my parents in the crowd.

"Hey!" I say, squeezing him in a hug first since he found me before anyone else did. He's standing with my adoptive parents, Park and Becca, who are next to Jett's parents, Bayleigh and Jace, and their daughter, Brooke. Brooke is a year younger than my brother. It's kind of a unique situation, but we're all one big happy family.

My parents swarm me next. Mom smells like her citrus perfume and coconut shampoo as she pulls me into a hug. "I'm so proud of you," she says, squeezing me.

"It took me long enough," I say, because I'm pretty sure everyone else is thinking it.

Dad steps up, hugging me next. "It doesn't matter how long it took," he says, smiling at me. "What matters is that you graduated. We're very proud of you."

His hair is graying on the sides. It seems a little grayer every time I look at him recently. He's in his early forties though, so it's not like he's old. My mom hides any evidence of gray hair with hair dye. Her auburn hair is shoulder-length now, and the shorter style suits her.

Jace and Bayleigh come over and hug me, with little Brooke wrapping her arms around my leg.

"So proud of you," Bayleigh says, kissing my cheek.

I thank them, and then look over at the man standing behind him. Jett has been here the whole time, watching, waiting for his turn. He looks so handsome in his black slim-fit pants and dark red Henley shirt. His normally dirty-blonde hair has morphed into a light brown recently, probably because he's only ever outside with a helmet or base-ball cap on and the sun no longer bleaches his hair.

His parents step back, and I walk forward, straight into his arms.

"Did you hear me cheering when they called your name?"

"I think everyone heard that," I say with a laugh.

Jett squeezes me in his arms. "Congrats, babe."

"Thank you."

"Who's hungry?" My father-in-law says.

The little kids immediately burst to life, declaring how hungry they are, followed by the adults. I've been so nervous all morning that I wasn't able to eat anything for breakfast. But now it's just after two in the afternoon, and I'm suddenly starving.

"Food sounds amazing," I say.

Jett's hand slides into mine. "Good thing I've got reservations at the best steakhouse in Texas."

Our two families pile into three cars and make the short drive to Taste of Texas, a well-known and slightly famous restaurant. They've been featured on TV shows for their food. It's pricey, but Jett refused to let me talk him into taking us somewhere cheaper. He said it's my graduation, and it should be celebrated in style.

The restaurant is gorgeous inside, and larger than it looks from the highway. The servers are dressed impeccably, and so well-trained that you feel like a celebrity when you walk in. Jett actually is kind of a celebrity around motocross towns, but I'm not. It's hard enough sometimes, just being the wife of a celebrity.

We're taken to a large table that fits all seven of us and we enjoy the most delicious meal ever. I'm not sure I've ever had anything so tasty. Even the garden salad was divine. My little brother and Jett's little sister are on their best behavior, which is really cute. It's been quite an adjustment with our little siblings running around. I was so used to being the only child in my family for so long, and so was Jett. He thought he'd be an only child forever, but then his parents had another baby a year after Bayleigh was a surrogate for my mom.

I love being a big sister, even if I am all grown up and live on my own with my husband. I still love coming back to their house and spending time with Elijah. Sometimes I don't want to be an adult. I just want to curl up under a blanket fort with my little brother and our parents and be happy, go-lucky kids in a great family. The kind of thing I never got to do when I was a kid.

But then other times, like now, when I'm sitting next to my husband at a fancy restaurant, watching him tell a story about his motocross racing team to our parents, I just feel so lucky. So incredibly lucky to have met these people and been taken in by them.

I got parents, and a family, and found the love of my life, all on accident.

And now, I'm a college graduate with a full-time job at the family business. I am so glad that college is over. And I'm so thrilled for the rest of my life to begin.

TWO
JETT

I'M SO full of steak and potatoes and buttery rolls. I ate so much food, I don't know if I'll ever be hungry again. Eh, strike that... I'm sure I'll be hungry in the morning. But dinner was amazing. I've been wanting to go to Taste of Texas ever since one of my dad's clients told me about it, but it's a fancy restaurant that requires reservations and I never seem to have a reason to go somewhere fancy. Until today. Keanna thought it was silly for me to reserve a dinner for her graduation, but I think it's the perfect reason to celebrate.

My wife is a college graduate. That's a pretty kick-ass accomplishment and I'm so proud of her. I hold back my smile as I watch her blow dry her hair after taking a shower. She'd only get annoyed and roll her eyes at me if she caught me smiling at her again. She thinks I'm making too big of a deal about her graduation, but I don't think I made a big enough deal about it.

She won't tell anyone, but she graduated with a perfect 4.0. I've watched her work so hard over the past few years, pouring over textbooks and writing papers and coming home from the university library with a dozen huge books for research. She studied, and worked hard, and still kept her full-time job at The Track. My wife is a freaking rock star and she's too humble to brag about it.

After we'd eaten dinner, the family had come over to our house to hang out a bit and eat the fancy bakery cake my mom and Becca had ordered. It was shaped like a graduation cap and had sparkly edible glitter on it. It was freaking delicious, and they let us keep the rest of it. I'm going to have a stomachache for days eating that thing.

Eventually, the family went home and Keanna took a shower, saying she wanted to scrub the stench of stadium off her. I think she just wanted some time alone to herself. She was stressed out about the whole graduation ceremony. She almost bailed on it a few times, but I knew how much it meant to her to walk across that stage, so I had encouraged her to go.

I'm glad she did. She seems happy about it. I'm just so proud of her. I want to rush across the bedroom and wrap her in a hug right this second, but then she'd probably laugh and push me away, saying she needs to finish drying her hair.

She has this habit of not being able to go to bed until her hair is perfectly, completely dry. These are the sort of things you only learn about your soul mate when you've been married for a little while. When Keanna washes her hair, she'll sit at her make up table thing (I think it's called a vanity?) and brush her hair and blow dry it for the longest time. If anything interrupts it, she'll be annoyed until she can get back and dry her hair.

And then there's me, who will shower, rub my head with a towel, and then pass out in bed with no worries whatsoever. Sure, I wake up with a mad case of bed-hair, but it doesn't bother me, probably because I wear a baseball cap or a dirt bike helmet all day.

I wonder what kinds of things Keanna thinks about me now that we're married? What are my quirks she finds endearing? Or annoying?

I bite my lip as I watch her dry her hair. I'm sitting on our bed, playing on my iPad. Our master bedroom is huge, so she feels really far away, even though she's just across the room. Hopefully she doesn't find me annoying at all. I don't find anything annoying about her. I adore every single inch of my wife, even her little quirks like needing super dry hair.

I guess I'm staring at her too long, because her eyes meet mine in her mirror. It's rectangular and bordered with lights. She'd called it a celebrity makeup mirror when we saw it in the furniture store.

"What?" she says, turning off the hair dryer.

I smile. "Nothing."

"You were staring at me like you're thinking something."

I shrug. She turns around in her chair so that she's looking directly at me instead of at my mirror reflection.

"I was just thinking about if you find me annoying."

She quirks an eyebrow. "Why would I find you annoying?"

"I dunno."

She rolls her eyes and turns back around to face the mirror.

"Did that annoy you?" I joke.

She snorts out a little laugh. "No... why? Do you think I'm annoying?"

I shake my head. "Not even a little bit."

She grins. "Good."

The hair dryer turns back on, so I glance down at my iPad and yawn. It's been a long day. We had to wake up early and drive an hour and a half to the big stadium the university uses for graduation. Keanna had to get there early since she's graduating, but I didn't want her to drive by herself, so I went early too and just hung out in my truck. Then graduation took a few hours, and then we hung out with our families. We've been busy all day, but only finally get to relax now.

I love married life.

I love being married to Keanna. I love watching her grow and challenge herself and accomplish hard things. She's such an inspiration. She works hard for what she has. Sometimes I feel like I don't have to work hard at all. Sure, I'm a professional motocross racer, but that's different. I was born into the motocross life. I grew up on a track and was trained by my dad, who was a professional himself. I kind of fell into this sport. I didn't have to work as hard for it as my Team Loco teammates did. And sometimes I feel guilty about it all. Like I'm here, living this amazing life, and like I don't deserve any of it. I feel like I didn't work hard enough for it.

The hair dryer shuts off and Keanna puts it back in the bathroom. A few moments later, she crawls into bed beside me, slipping down into the sheets and then snuggling up next to my arm.

She sighs. "Ugh. I'm not tired anymore."

I chuckle and set my iPad on the nightstand. "It was a long, exciting day. I feel exhausted but not exactly sleepy."

"Same here." She rolls over on her back, lacing her fingers together over her stomach while she stares at the ceiling. "I can't believe I finally graduated. I thought the day would never come."

"I did," I say. "You worked hard for it and you deserve it."

She glances over at me. "Do you think it's kind of a waste?"

"What do you mean?"

She shrugs, her gaze turning back up toward the ceiling. "Like... I have my job at The Track. And I don't want to work anywhere else. So it's not like I'm required to get a degree... I just wanted one. Feels kind of like a waste of money."

"No way. You're educated now," I say playfully, nudging her with my elbow. "You know all kinds of smarty pants business stuff. Stuff I don't understand. That will only make you an even better employee."

She considers it for a moment. "Yeah, I guess you're right."

I shuffle down in the bed, turning to snuggle up against her back. My hand slides down her waist, stopping on her hip. I have the sudden urge to tickle her here because I know she'll squirm and it's the cutest thing, but I hold back. I lean forward and kiss her neck.

"I'm so proud of you."

"Thanks..." she says softly.

I cuddle with her until her breathing slows and she drifts off to sleep and I remind myself for the millionth time that I am the luckiest man in the world.

THREE
KEANNA

THE ABSOLUTE BEST part of graduating college isn't the diploma. It's the freedom. For the first time since Jett and I have been together, I'm finally getting to travel with him for an entire motocross racing season. I've tried in the past but never had time, and while I've gone with him to a few races every so often, I've never been able to be with him for the whole thing. Until now. I'm so excited I could burst.

The professional motocross racing season takes place every summer. It's twelve races at twelve different famous motocross tracks across the country. And these tracks are incredible. They're decades old, ultra-famous, and basically legends in the world of motocross. On the whole scale of things, our business, The Track, is still a fairly new track and while we host plenty of amateur races here, we've never had a professional race. This is the big leagues. The best you can get in the professional motocross world.

It's also a lot of work. The races start in May and end in September, and some are once a week, some have a week or two off between the races. So we'll be flying or driving somewhere twelve times, staying for a day or two each time, and then coming home between. It makes for a super hectic schedule when you're stuck at home working and your husband is off traveling. But with Jett and I together, I think it'll be a lot of fun. Plus, I'll get to see the other Team Loco girlfriends. Or fiancés, I should say. Two of Jett's teammates are engaged, and I couldn't be more excited. Since Jett races as a member of Team Loco, we're all kind of a little family.

I love getting to hang out with the other girl-friends because they get me more than my other friends get me. They all know what it's like being with a guy who is famous in his sport and has tons of fans who wish he was still single. The last two years have been difficult because I've been working full time at The Track and also going to school for my degree. I didn't get to watch Jett race at all the last two years, not even when they came to Houston for the supercross race, which is the closest venue near us. But now that's all about to change. I am so excited to spend this summer racing schedule with my husband. And all his jealous fans can just get over it.

It's mid-morning on Saturday, and Jett and I are eating breakfast. He made us pancakes and bacon this morning, and I'm sitting at the kitchen table just enjoying my morning while he watches an extreme sports talk show thing on the TV. I don't know how some people love watching so-called experts talk about sports, but Jett loves it. Probably because every now and then they talk about him.

We leave on Thursday for the first race of the season which takes place in Pala, California. I'll be at work Monday through Wednesday, and then I'm off. Mom and Bayleigh thought about hiring a part time employee to cover my shifts, but then they decided that they can probably handle my work while I'm gone. While my mom and Jett's mom used to run The Track back in the original days, lately I've been running it much more often and they only work part time. The Track is almost twenty-five years old now, with thousands of loyal clients, and it runs like a well-oiled machine.

My phone beeps while I'm reaching for another piece of bacon. Jett always cooks up a pack of bacon and then puts it all on a plate in the middle of the table. Sometimes we fight over the last piece, but I usually let him have it because he eats way more than I do. I pick up my phone and see a text from my mom, Becca.

Mom: where are the blank envelopes?

Me: bottom drawer on the far left of the office.

Mom: okay and what about the stamps?

Me: I print them online.

Mom: You... what? How am I supposed to do that!?

I chuckle, shaking my head as I type out a reply.

Me: I doubt you'll need many stamps while I'm gone but I'll print out a bunch before I leave.

Mom: Okay cool. Do you need a suitcase? I have that nice new one you can borrow.

Me: No thanks, we're good. Jett has enough suitcases for the both of us, lol

Mom: awesome! Let me know if you need anything. By the way, how do I update the social media pages?

Me: I'll take care of that... no worries.

Mom: you're the best

I roll my eyes and set the phone down.

"What is it?" Jett asks.

I take a bite of bacon. "Mom is freaking out about running The Track while I'm gone. She acts like she didn't run the place herself years ago," I say with a laugh.

"Well, you've taken the business to a whole new level," he says, taking a sip of coffee. "I think both of our moms would be totally lost without you."

"Hopefully they'll survive for twelve weeks because nothing is stopping me from going with you to these races."

"Hell yeah." He grins, then looks down at his coffee cup and frowns when he finds it empty. He gets up and pops a coffee pod into the coffee maker to brew another cup.

It occurs to me that I haven't told him about the

thing I've been daydreaming of for months. I've kept it to myself because I wanted to keep it as a sort of gift to myself after graduating. Also, I don't know how he'll take it. He might think it's a terrible idea, or maybe he'll love it. All I know, is I really, really hope he agrees.

"Babe?" I say as the coffee maker gurgles and grinds, pouring hot coffee into his mug, which was a free gift from a Team Loco banquet we went to a while back. It has the racing team's logo on the cup.

"You want some coffee?" he asks.

I shake my head. "I actually wanted to talk to you about something."

"Uh oh," he says with a grin. "Is it bad?"

"Not if you like dogs."

He quirks an eyebrow and sits back down at the table next to me. "What do you mean?"

"I want a dog."

"Really?"

I nod. "A puppy. Like, when we get back from the summer motocross season and I go back to work... I'd like to get a puppy and then train him to be a good dog and take him to work and stuff."

"That sounds amazing," Jett says, stirring some milk into his coffee. "I love dogs. I've never really had time to raise one before."

"Right? But after I spend the summer with you, I feel like I'll have more time to take care of a dog. I'm out of school, so even when you're busy with racing, I can still take care of him."

Jett's face lights up as we talk about it, and I can tell he's getting just as excited about the idea as I am. "What kind of dog do you want?"

I shrug. "I don't know. A puppy, for sure. But just any breed. I figure we should adopt one from the animal shelter and give it a good home."

He nods. "I'm down with that."

I clap my hands together. "I'm so excited!"

Jett smiles at me for a long moment. "Me, too."

After breakfast, I get started packing my stuff for the race next weekend. It's still a few days away, but I want to be prepared. I check the weather for that part of California and find it'll be sunny and a little cool, so I pack clothes accordingly. We'll be there three days, one for practice, one for the race, and one to travel back home. I'm so eager to be prepared for the trip that I pack seven outfits. Then I wonder if maybe that's too many, but then I keep them in my suitcase because you can never have too many clothes. Maybe we'll go somewhere nice for dinner, so I'll need a nice outfit. And maybe I'll spill my food all over myself and need another outfit. Yep, more is better.

Jett walks into our bedroom with his iPad in his hand.

"I've made a terrible mistake," he says, eyes wide. "I looked up an online pet adoption website."

"Why is that bad?" I ask.

He sighs. "I suddenly want to adopt every dog in the world."

I laugh and toss a sock at him. He catches it with one hand and then returns it to my open sock drawer. "Now I'm just bummed that we have to wait twelve weeks to get our new little furry best friend."

"Well, we can't get a puppy while you're racing all over the country," I say, leaning up on my toes to kiss him. "But twelve weeks will be over before we know it."

"And hopefully I'll be a championship winner," he says, sliding his hands around my waist. He yanks me closer to him, his rock-hard body pressing rigidly against my much softer body. I giggle as he trails kisses down my neck, to my collarbone.

"Why are you packing?" he says, seemingly noticing my open suitcase on the bed for the first time since he walked in here.

"Because we're going to California," I say sarcastically.

"In like, a week," he says with a snort.

"It's in four days," I say, placing a hand on my hip. "I'm just being prepared."

"You know I always just toss clothes into a suitcase the day before I leave, right?"

I roll my eyes. "You can get away with that because you're a guy and guys look sexy in anything."

"You look sexy in nothing," he says without missing a beat. He looks me up and down appraisingly, and the look in his eyes tells me he likes what he sees.

I grin, then I shove the suitcase off the bed to make room for what comes next.

FOUR

JETT

EVEN AFTER A LIFETIME of racing dirt bikes, and years spent on a professional racing team, I'm still full of nervous energy the day before the race. I know I'm prepared, well-trained, in shape, and feeling great. I shouldn't stress, but I will anyway. It's the first race of the summer motocross season. How I perform on the first race sets the expectations for the rest of the season. Last season, the sports reporters said Jett Adams was racing lazy, like someone who just thought they could coast their way through from week to week. I refuse to let them say that about me this year.

Keanna and I have a nine a.m. flight to California, so we're here at the Houston Intercontinental Airport bright and early. We haven't traveled anywhere together in so long, and I'm more than grateful to have her with me here today. I travel constantly as a professional racer and I'm always leaving Houston alone, meeting up with my team-mates later on since they live in different states. It's nice not being alone, but it's even better having my wife with me.

I hold her hand while we each roll our suitcases beside us.

"Ooh, coffee!" I say as we approach the Star-bucks inside the airport. I'm still half-asleep and caffeine sounds like magic right now. "What do you want, Babe?"

She curls her lip. "I don't want anything."

"It's coffee," I say, wiggling my eyebrows. "It's the elixir of angels."

She snorts. "I'm scared it'll make me pee."

I lift an eyebrow curiously.

She shrugs, her cheeks turning a bit pink. "I'm scared I'll have to pee on the plane," she says quietly so no one overhears.

"There are bathrooms on the plane."

"Yeah, but..." She makes a face. "They're scary. And I don't want to get up and walk down the aisle while everyone watches me." She shakes her head as if the image in her mind is the worst thing she's thought all day. "I know I'm a weirdo."

"You're my weirdo," I say, pulling her in for a kiss. "If you don't want coffee, do you mind if I get it?"

"Be my guest," she says, stepping to the side so I can walk toward the coffee line.

My coffee is piping hot and delicious. I always grab a large Americano from this airport Starbucks when I'm here alone. Arriving at the airport two hours early is such a drag. Keanna and I make our way to the security checkpoints, getting in line behind dozens of other passengers. I never have to worry when I'm here in Houston. Most people don't even bother looking at me, and those that do don't recognize me.

But California airports are a little different. It's not like I'm some epic celebrity on a famous TV show —the whole world doesn't know who I am. Just people who follow motocross know me, and there seems to be way more of those people in Cali. I usually get at least three fans following me around the airports there. I'm hoping and praying that doesn't happen this summer while Keanna is with me.

"I've been thinking of puppy names," Keanna

says while we wait in the uncomfortable plastic chairs just outside of our terminal.

"Oh yeah? What have you got?"

She leans back in her chair, resting her feet on top of her suitcase. "I was thinking something dirt bike related...like maybe Kawi or Honda for a girl."

"Or Braap for a boy," I say.

She quirks an eyebrow. "Um, no. That's dumb."

"Braap is a cool name!"

She grins, shaking her head. "No, it's not."

"Hmm, okay what about...Moto?"

She considers it. "That's a cute name."

"You could even bring the puppy to work with you," I say, sipping my coffee. "Let him be the work mascot."

She nods. "For sure. I can't wait."

After what feels like forever, we're finally on the plane. My coffee is long gone and I'm craving some more, so I can't wait until our flight attendant comes by so I can get more caffeine. Keanna quickly falls asleep after the plane takes off, and I sit next to her watching a show on my phone while her head rests on my shoulder.

An hour or so goes by and Keanna jolts awake suddenly. Her eyes widen and she puts one hand over her mouth and one on her stomach.

"What's wrong?" I say.

"I don't feel good." She takes a deep breath, looking up at the ceiling, then slowly exhales. "I feel carsick or something." She cracks half a smile. "I guess that would be airsick."

The fact that she's making jokes makes me feel a little better. Still, I don't want to have some kind of medical emergency while on a plane far away from hospitals.

"What's all wrong?" I say, touching her forehead. She doesn't seem to have a fever. "What hurts?"

She shrugs my worries off with a shake of her head. "I just feel nauseous. It's probably nerves."

"Why are you nervous?" I ask.

She looks me in the eyes, a sudden bashful frown on her face. "I dunno. It's just nerve-wracking to be with you for the races. All the fans will be annoying, and then I'm also nervous for you because I don't want you to get hurt or anything. Plus, I want you to win."

I reach for her hand. Her face pales and now I suddenly know why that one emoji that's making a face like its sick is green. She kind of looks green right now.

"Babe, what's wrong?"

"I think I'm going to throw up."

And just like that, she jumps up and practically leaps over my legs to get out of our seat row. In a frantic rush, she scurries up the aisle and into the airplane bathroom. Her biggest fear come to life. I wish I could be there with her, but I'm pretty sure the flight attendants would frown on me running into the same tiny bathroom. Keanna has her phone with her so I text her quickly letting her know I'm here if she needs me.

Key: I just puked and now I feel better.

Me: Are you coming out soon?

Key: ugh, I don't want to. I hate airplane bathrooms!

Me: Want me to meet you and walk back with you?

Key: No... that would be even more embarrassing. Give me a minute.

The minute she requests turns into ten more minutes. Finally, she returns, slipping quickly into her seat and then fishing gum from her purse. "Gross," she says as she unwraps a piece of gum. "I mean, there was nothing in my stomach but I couldn't stop dry heaving."

"I hope you're not getting sick."

"Nah," she says, shaking her head. "I'm just nervous."

I reach over and hold her hand. I'd take away all of her bad feelings if I could. I'd feel them a thousand times worse if it meant she never had to worry about anything. But life doesn't work that way. So I just hold on to her hand and tell her I love her.

FIVE
KEANNA

I CAN'T BELIEVE I'm such a mess. It's just a flight to California. It's not a big deal! And yet my stomach feels so twisted and nauseated and my heart is fluttering. My whole body is just one massive ball of anxiety. I've spent years wanting to travel with Jett for an entire motocross season and here I am freaking out about it instead of being grateful and enjoying the moment. I can't believe my brain is being so horrible to me. I need to get it together!

I manage to go the rest of the flight without puking again, and now I'm wishing I had gotten a coffee because I'm exhausted and coffee sounds amazing. I ended up needing to rush to the airplane bathroom anyhow... so my plan to avoid it didn't even work. Blah.

When our plan lands and we step out into the terminal, my heart races again. The place is filled with people just going about their business, but I can't stop the mental images of Jett's fanatic fangirls rushing up and bombarding him.

That doesn't happen, though.

No one even pays attention to us. We brought our luggage as carry-ons, so we don't need to wait by the baggage claim. Jett and I wheel our suitcases through the terminal and all the way down to the exit and not a single person looks our way. I'm so relieved, I feel weightless as we step into a taxi.

Jett ends up chatting with our taxi driver on the short commute to the hotel that Team Loco has arranged for us to stay in. He tells him about his race this weekend, and the two men chat happily while I sit here staring out the window. I guess I thought California would be a lot different looking. I feel silly, because images of Hollywood and movie stars fill my head when I think of this west coast state, but really California is a lot like Texas in that it's huge. There's more here than just celebrities.

We're in Pala, which is a small, mostly Native American community located at the southern tip of California. The air is cooler and less humid than I'm used to back at home. When we arrive at the hotel, I step outside into the sunshine and gorgeous weather and take a deep breath. Mountains line the horizon. We definitely don't have mountains in Lawson, Texas.

"How are you feeling?" Jett says, one hand resting gently on my back. We're standing in the parking lot as the taxi drives away, and I've been so overtaken by the beauty of this town that I almost don't hear what he just said.

"I'm good," I say. "Hungry."

He chuckles. "Me too. Let's go find the guys."

The rest of the Team Loco guys are already here, having arrived a few hours before we did. Jett and I check into our hotel room, then he texts them and we agree to meet up in the lobby so we can go find a place to grab lunch together.

Zach Pena steps out of an elevator at the same time we step out of ours. He's a muscular guy who sometimes acts half his age. He's always got some kind of fidget spinner with him. Today, he's holding a yellow yo-yo, which he drops and pulls up as he walks over to us.

"Hey Mrs. Adams," he says with his Tennessee twang as he pulls me into a hug. He smells like coconut body wash and I wonder if he stole that from his girlfriend, Bree because it doesn't really smell like something I think he'd buy for himself. "Glad to have you here."

"Glad to be here," I say after he releases me from his massive hug.

Clay Summers and Aiden Strauss step off the elevator together. Jett gives them all bro-hugs, as I like to call them, and they smack each other around playfully like the grown children they are.

"Key!" Aiden says, sauntering over to me with that rich-boy swagger of his. I know he tries to hide it, but he grew up wealthy and it's obvious. He's not one of those rich jerks, though. He's cool. He gives me a hug. "Finally," he says, looking up to the sky quickly. "Finally Jett's girl gets to watch him race. We've missed you."

"Yeah, we missed you, but not Jett," Clay says, pulling me in for a hug next. "Jett can keep his ass at home next time. Maybe give the rest of us a chance to win, eh?"

"You wish man," Jett playfully snaps back.

Clay pulls back and holds onto my arms as he appraises me. He's really tall, with dark hair shaved short and tons of tattoos. Of the four of members of Team Loco, Clay is the most intimidating. He's also the most observant. "You doing okay? You look a little off."

"Just really anxious," I say quiet enough for only us to hear.

"Worried about your man?" Clay says as we walk behind the guys on our way out of the hotel. "Because you shouldn't be. Jett's been riding really well lately. He's got this series in the bag, if you ask me."

I shake my head. "Not really worried about him. It's just nerve-wracking, being the wife of the guy so many other women want."

"Ah," he says with a head nod that shows me he gets it. "Avery and the other girls will be here tomorrow. You can stick together as a united front that tells the jealous fan girls to ef off."

I grin. "That sounds like a great idea."

SIX

JETT

WE'RE two races into the summer motocross season and everything is going great. I've started off on a hot streak, winning both races with my teammates taking the other two podium finishes. We're riding hard, getting stronger each day, and our bikes are running fast and smoothly. We have the best mechanics on Team Loco, that's for sure. They work hard to keep our bikes ready for each race.

It's even better having Keanna with me. Once she met up with the other Team Loco girlfriends, she's been in a much better mood. She doesn't seem so nervous anymore because together, they're like their own team. They can face the fangirls as one united front. Plus, Keanna doesn't have to be left alone while I'm at the races. We have practice, then the race, and of course all the autograph signing before and after each race. All the work I have to do means she's left alone most days, but at least the girls all have each other.

Right now we're on the east coast in Mt. Morris, Pennsylvania, in the stressful hours before the High Point National race. We've already practiced once this morning, and now my team and I are lined up behind a plastic table, signing posters of ourselves for the fans. Behind us is our Team Loco motorhome, and to the right is a large Team Loco canopy tent with all of our dirt bikes on display.

In front of me is a long line of fans. My signature has become refined over the years. The first few times I had to sign autographs, I signed *Jett Adams* the usual way I sign my name—with each letter spelled out. But after a dozen autographs that way, you start getting sloppier. It's not even because I'm lazy or anything—it's necessary. I can't sign a hundred autographs minutes before I go race because then my hand muscles will be too sore. Now my official signature is a J and an A with some squiggles between the two.

I grab another poster and sign it for the small boy standing across from the table. He's grinning from ear to ear, watching me. "Here you go," I say, handing it over.

"Thank you!" he says before turning to look at his mom with a big, silly grin.

I smile back. The kids are the best part of doing the whole "meet the fans" thing. They're innocent and kind and have no ill-intentions. They're all little mini dirt bike fans with dreams of going pro one day. And who knows? Maybe they will be here racing one day when they're older. That's how it happened for me.

"Incoming," Zach whispers from beside me. I'm still smiling at the little kid, but when I look up, I realize what he was warning me about. Two younger women, probably around my age, are walking toward me with matching expressions on their faces that instantly make my stomach tighten. It's hard to describe the look of someone who is about to annoy you, but my gut instinct is never wrong on this.

One of the women has long brown hair and the other has blonde hair in a ponytail. They both wear matching cut-off jean shorts and and a Team Loco T-shirt. It's the kind of shirt you can buy at the merchandise booths each season. The back has a list of all twelve races on it.

Now, I don't normally get upset when fans walk

AMY SPARLING

up to see me. After all, this is literally the meet-and-greet hour before the races begin. But what bothers me is how one of them is holding a cell phone in that classic way that tells me she's recording me as they approach.

I hate being recorded.

Unless it's a professional TV camera filming me race around a motocross track, a commercial I'm being paid to participate in, or a silly social media video with my wife, I don't want to be on film.

"Jett Adams!" the girl without the phone says in a bubbly voice. "The famous Jett Adams!"

"That's me," I say, tapping my Sharpie pen on the table. "Would you like an autograph?"

"Um, yes!" she says. It's like she's trying to imitate Alexis Rose on the TV show Schitt's Creek. "I would love an autograph but I'd really like a moment of your time."

"I want one, too!" the girl with the phone in my face says.

I bite back my annoyance and focus on signing my name to two of the posters in front of me. Then I cap the marker and lift up the posers, holding them out to the two ladies. The phone is still in my face.

"Jett, I'm Marissa," the first girl says, flashing her eyelashes at me. She doesn't reach for the posters. It's

40

clear she wants to stay here a while, which is not only annoying, it's rude to the rest of the people in line. Beside me, my other three teammates keep signing autographs for fans while I'm stuck here talking to these women.

"How can I help you?" I say, my voice clipped and my expression neutral. I'm not in the mood to chat with someone who happily puts a camera in my face without asking permission.

"You're the only married member of Team Loco, and you're still so young," she says, glancing to the camera as she says it.

"That's not a question."

She laughs and reaches for the poster I just signed. "My question is, don't you think you jumped into marriage a little too soon?"

"Nope."

I turn toward the people standing in line behind her, but she doesn't get the hint because she and her friend are still standing here.

"We think you got married too soon, Jett," she says. "We think you got forced into a marriage you didn't want and now you're trapped."

Anger bubbles up in my chest. I want to tell this woman off. I want to yell at her and tell her to mind her own business and never talk to me again. But people are watching, and I have a reputation to uphold. Plus, being kind to fans is literally in my contract with Team Loco.

"This is an autograph session," I say, sliding both posters toward them.

"No, it's a meet and greet," Marissa says, smiling at the camera before turning her gaze back on me.

"You can both move along now so the other fans can have a chance to get an autograph. Pretty sure no one else is here to start needless drama."

I brace myself for backlash because I shouldn't have been so rude just now, but nothing bad happens. They just take their posters and walk off and I breathe a sigh of relief. Just when I think the public might have finally gotten over my decision to get married without asking their permission first, something like this happens. I wish people only cared about my racing statistics, not my personal life.

"Good thing Keanna is in the motor home," Zach says. "I wouldn't want her to hear that shit."

"Same," I say. I take a deep breath and put on a fake smile for the father-son duo that approaches our table next. Clay, Aiden, Zach, and I all sign posters for the kid who thanks us profusely. When they walk away, I turn to Zach.

"Never get married. The fans won't ever let you live it down."

"That's true," he says. "They won't. But that's not going to stop me from marrying Bree."

I don't blame him, obviously. We have to do what makes us happy, even if it means annoying the fans. "Maybe the fans will turn on you next and forget about me," I say.

He snorts. "Doubtful. They loooooove you."

<hr>

I'M STILL PUMPED from the post-race adrenaline as I walk down the carpeted hallway of our hotel. I didn't win tonight—Aiden swooped in and passed me on the last lap—but any win for Team Loco is still a win in my book. We're spending one more night here and then flying back home in the morning. We'll get a two week break at home before head to Michigan for the Red Bud National race in July. I'm ready for a two week break where we can just relax at home and I can work out and prepare for the rest of the season. All this traveling week to week is draining.

Finding a hotel's ice machine is sometimes a unique adventure. Some hotels have them clearly marked, and have one on each floor. Others make you go to the lobby. This hotel has one on every other floor, so I jog down the stairs and fill up our ice bucket. Keanna is back at our hotel, having found a baking show on the TV that she loves watching.

After the ice plunks into the bucket, I head back upstairs only to see Marcus making his way to my hotel room.

"Marcus?" I call out so he doesn't knock on the door and scare Keanna. Marcus is Team Loco's business manager. He's a former racer himself, but now in his "old" age of mid-forty-something, he's retired from the racing aspect of the sport and now manages us.

He's still dressed in khaki pants and a blue button up shirt, the business attire he wears at the races when there's some bigwig in the industry he's trying to impress. Most of the time, the guy is in jeans and T-shirts. It's just after nine o'clock at night, so I wonder why he hasn't changed clothes yet.

Marcus turns around after I call his name. "We need to talk."

My stomach drops. "What's going on?"

Marcus runs a hand through his dark hair. As I get closer, it's obvious that he looks exhausted. He probably hasn't had time to shower yet and that's why he's still dressed like that so late at night.

"I've just had my ass handed to me by corporate, all because of you."

I stop, the ice bucket freezing my hand. "What the hell for?"

"The video two fans posted online today that shows you acting in a way very unbecoming of your Team Loco contract."

It takes me a second to realize what he's talking about, but then I remember the women who recorded me at the last race. "That's crap, and you know it," I say. "I was minding my own business, being a good team member signing autographs and they accosted me."

"I know, but your reaction was what corporate considers rude, and they're pissed. They wanted to punish you by pulling you from the rest of the racing season."

"What?" My voice booms down the hallway.

Marcus holds out a hand to calm me. "I talked them down to three races."

"What?" I say again, slightly less angry this time, but I'm still pissed."

"Sorry, kid," Marcus says, shaking his head like he agrees this is all bullshit. "Conduct is a big deal

45

since we're supposed to be a *family sport*." He rolls his eyes. "The best I could do was three races."

"I seriously have to go back home for two months just because I politely told some women to leave my wife alone?"

"It wasn't very polite," he says.

I groan. "How am I supposed to act when stuff like that happens?"

Marcus shrugs. "Honestly, I'm not sure. Just smile and be nice, I guess. And whatever you do, never be rude or even remotely close to rude."

"This is so wrong," I say, gritting my teeth. "They're insulting my wife, to my face."

"You want to swap places with one of the thousands of other wannabe racers who would kill to be in your place?"

My jaw tightens, but I don't reply.

Marcus claps me on the shoulder. "That's what I thought. Goodnight."

I take a deep breath, closing my eyes for a moment before going back to my hotel room. I hope Keanna didn't hear any of that. I hope she doesn't know anything about what happened. Of course, how am I supposed to keep it a secret if I can't race for the next three races? She'll find out eventually.

But maybe we can have this one last night together before she learns of the drama.

I pull out my key card and unlock the hotel room door. When I step inside, Keanna is sitting up on the bed, laptop in front of her. The look on her face tells me one thing.

She already knows.

SEVEN
KEANNA

"IT'S FINE," I say.

Jett's hair is tussled, probably from anxiously running his hands through it out in the hallway. I could hear the deep tone of Marcus' voice out there, but that wasn't the first clue I got that some new Internet drama was going down. Social media notifications started blowing up my phone a couple hours ago. I always get a bunch of notifications on race days, usually from fans congratulating me on Jett's win, but when there were more notifications than usual today, I assumed it had been because he'd come in second place instead of first.

I had assumed wrong.

Some lady with a YouTube channel called Marissa's Motocross Musings decided to put my husband on blast today in a poorly edited video she uploaded probably minutes after recording Jett at the meet-and-greet session. Seriously, she could have taken some time to edit in some commentary or even post a picture of me taken at a bad angle to make me look ugly, like other fangirls do. But I guess she was just so excited to upload her juicy content that she couldn't wait.

It's a short video, taken by someone holding a phone up to Jett's face. They try talking crap about me but he tells them off. And then the women walk away and the camera turns to Marissa, who goes on a five minute rant about how I stole Jett from the motocross community and how he's much more attractive than I am and he could get any woman he wants and yet he's stuck with me. Then she and her friend proceed to talk about how he probably cheats on me constantly because he's too hot to be kept locked down by one woman. Then she grinned at the camera and said, "Ladies, make your move! That ring on his finger doesn't mean a thing!"

Ugh.

Stuff like this used to really bother me. So much that I'd question my relationship with Jett. I'd start thinking I wasn't good enough for him, and I'd think I should just break up with him so he can go find a better person to live his life with. But Jett has reassured me time and time again that I am the woman for him. Plus, it helps that I'm friends with the other Team Loco girlfriends. They go through similar drama. The thing is, fans are mean. But those two women today aren't really fans in my opinion. They're just mean, bitter, hateful people. Because I happen to have a huge crush on a handful of sexy celebrity actors, but that doesn't mean I hate their spouses. If anything, I'm happy for their spouses because they're living life with a sexy man who loves them. Just like me.

Real fans of Jett are happy for him. I can't stop hateful people form being hateful. All I can do is hold my head high and let their nastiness roll off my back.

Jett runs one hand through his hair as he enters the hotel room, setting the ice bucket on the nearby table. "Really? You sure you're okay?"

"Are you okay?" I say, patting the bed beside me.

"No."

My eyes widen. That's not exactly the answer I was expecting. Jett never lets this stuff get to him. Usually he's comforting me instead of the other way around. "Babe, it's okay," I say, smiling up at him.

He sits next to me and exhales a long, pained

sigh. "I mean, it will be okay, but right now I'm pretty pissed."

"It's not a big deal," I say, touching his arm. "Just two mean people saying mean things. Who cares?"

"I care, because it got me suspended."

A cold slice of anger shoots through my chest. *"What?"*

He nods, lips pressed in a tight line. "Marcus just said corporate wanted to suspend me for the rest of the season but he talked them into three races."

I'm so angry I can't even think of anything to say. I breathe in through my nose, teeth gritted together. "That's four races," I say softly, anger seeping into my words.

He nods, knowing what I mean. Three suspended races plus the one today that he didn't win. That's four out of twelve for the whole season, which means even if he comes back and wins the rest of the races, it probably won't be enough to give him an overall season win. He'll drop down in the rankings. He might even lose sponsors because of this.

"I'm going to make my own YouTube channel," I say indignantly. "I'll call it Keanna's Motocross Musings. First episode: Marissa is a bitch."

Jett snorts out a laugh. "Now that would be hilarious."

I grin, leaning over until my head rests on his shoulder. "Of course, I'd probably get even more hate and then I'd end up getting you fired, but it's fun to daydream about being able to tell Marissa exactly what I think about her."

"We'll take the high road and ignore her," he says with a sigh. "It's not fun on the high road."

"No, but at least we're on it together."

We sit here in contemplative silence for a few moments, my head on his shoulder, the hotel television softly playing in the background. Jett breathes in deeply then slowly exhales.

"I can't race again for another month. What are we going to do for a whole month?"

"I'll just go back to work," I say, looking up at him. "You'll have to sit in our bedroom and think about what you did."

"For a whole month?" he jokes.

I nod, pretending to be serious. "Yep. And your punishment for getting in trouble with Team Loco is that you have to clean the house. And cook me dinner every day."

"I already do those things."

"And give me foot massages."

He laughs. "Okay. I accept my punishment."

I slide back on the bed and lift my feet, placing them in his lap. "Get to work, mister."

IN THE MORNING, I wake up to the smell of a hot coffee cup sitting on my nightstand and the sound of the shower water running. Jett must have woken up early and gone down to the hotel lobby for the coffee. I sit up and take a sip, but it's still so hot it's scalding so I set the coffee back down and venture across the small hotel room. He's left the bathroom door slightly open while the shower water runs.

I peak inside and see Jett brushing his teeth, wearing just a pair of boxers. He sees me in the mirror reflection and winks. I slip into the bathroom and decide to brush my teeth too, so I don't have morning breath. When I've finished, Jett is checking the temperature of the shower water.

"This place takes forever to get hot water," he complains.

"I can think of something to do while we wait," I say, batting my eyelashes at him.

His expression turns sultry, those gorgeous eyes of his making my knees week. "Oh yeah?"

I nod and move forward, sliding my hands up his bare chest and hooking my fingers together behind his neck. We kiss, slow and soft, as if we have all the time in the world. I'm pretty sure we need to leave for our flight in less than an hour, so we actually need to make this quick. But Jett's kisses make you want to get lost in them forever. I can easily lose hours just making out with him.

I draw in a breath trying to steady myself so I can tell him we need to be quick so we don't miss our flight. His head dips and he kisses my neck, sending a shooting zap of lust throw my whole body. Now I don't really care if we miss the flight. It's not like we have anywhere to be for the next month... maybe we should just stay here in each other's arms until he gets to race again.

"I love you," he whispers with his lips against my neck.

"I love you more," I say back. Well, I attempt to say it. I gasp right in the middle when he kisses me again.

And then, just he's about to lift my shirt off, it hits me. That awful nauseated feeling I got on the plane.

"Oh no."

I step back, pushing him away from me, shaking

my head in horror and fear of what's about to happen next.

"You gotta go."

"What? What's wrong?" He reaches for my hand but I shrug him away.

"Please go," I say, pushing him toward the bathroom door. "I'm about to puke and I don't want you to see it."

He looks so concerned. So serious. So caring. But none of that matters because I am not about to puke in front of my husband. Gross. I shove him out the door and close it quickly behind him.

Then I get sick for the next fifteen minutes.

EIGHT

JETT

I KNOW most people enjoy a good vacation away from work, but I personally hate it. I do spend almost every day of my month-long hiatus riding at my family track, but it doesn't bring me much joy. The thing is, I've grown up here on this track, and I know all three separate motocross tracks in their entirety. I've ridden them so many thousands of times that there's no challenge for me. I could probably ride my dirt bike to the starting line, close my eyes and take off, doing a whole lap without ever looking.

I mean, I won't because that sounds super dangerous, but I bet I could.

So while I spend my suspension at the track making sure I stay in shape and ride a lot, it's so boring I want to scream. The only good thing is being with Keanna each day, hanging out with her while she does her day job at The Track's front office. I bought her a beautiful frame from her diploma from her university, and it finally arrives in the mail after a few weeks. It's wooden with a metal emblem of the school's logo on it and the thing was nearly three hundred dollars. I'm not sure it's worth that much money, but it looks great. We frame her diploma and hang it up in her office at The Track.

Don't get me wrong, I love spending time with my wife, but I wish we were spending time together out at the races with the rest of my team, instead of stuck here in Lawson, Texas with nothing much to do.

On the three race days I'm forced to skip, I try not to spend all day refreshing my phone to see what the world is saying about my absence. But then during the races, I park in front of the TV and watch the entire thing on the edge of my seat. Aiden wins the Red Bud national the first week I'm gone, and then Clay wins Southwick with Aiden just right on his heel and Zach behind him. But the Spring Creek National in Millville is a disaster. Zach's front tire pops halfway through the race, putting him out of finishing. Aiden collides with a Team Yamaha racer at the starting line and it takes both of them two full laps to get their bikes started again, putting them far behind in the race. Clay is the only Team Loco member still in the running, and the pressure must get to him because he finishes in third place, with two other rookies on other teams beating him.

It's a disaster. I feel like I've let my whole team down because everything falls apart when I'm not there. And sure, the tire popping isn't exactly my fault but I still wish I had been there for my team. So I'm more than ready to go back when my three race suspension is over. Keanna is even more nervous as we drive to the airport. I reach over and take her hand.

"You feeling okay?"

She nods quickly. "I haven't eaten anything in eighteen hours so there's no way I'll throw up."

I frown. "What if we cancel the flight and charter a private plane instead?"

Her eyes widen. "That'd be really expensive."

I shrug. "Would you feel more comfortable?"

She considers it for a minute. "No. I think I'd be upset you spent so much money," she says with a laugh. The she smiles up at me. "I'm fine. I haven't felt sick in a couple of weeks."

"Hmm..." I get a weird feeling as she reminds me

that she hasn't been sick lately. She was only sick when we were traveling.

"What?" she says.

"You only got sick when we were traveling for the races. And since we've been home, you've been fine."

"Okay..." she says, waiting for me to continue.

"Well..." I shrug my shoulders while I drive. "I feel like maybe you're so nervous about being at the races that it's making you sick."

"I don't know..." She looks out the window. "Maybe."

"Would you rather stay home?" I ask, squeezing her hand. "It won't hurt my feelings."

"No, I want to be with you. I've waited so long to get to travel with you."

"But if it's making you sick... maybe you shouldn't do it."

She sits up straighter and shakes her head. "No way. I'm fine, babe. I promise. I feel great."

I'm still not entirely sure I believe that, but I don't want to argue. If she wants to come with me, I'm more than happy to have her. But when we get to the airport, I skip the Starbucks and don't mention anything about food or drinks just so she won't feel bad about what happened last time.

We make it through the entire flight just fine. Keanna and I sync up our Bluetooth headphones and watch the same TV show on my iPad for the whole flight to Washington. This weekend's race takes place in Washougal, a gorgeous track that I love racing on. Keanna is telling me all about some girlie TV show she and her mom have been obsessed with lately while we take the taxi to our hotel, and yeah, I'll admit, I kind of zone out for a few minutes because Keanna's voice is so soothing and she's talking about a show that I don't really care about. Sometimes I just like hearing her voice.

I glance out the window at the tall pine trees and gorgeous northwestern landscape and it suddenly hits me that we're in Washington. Home of Forks, Washington which is where Twilight took place. That's Keanna's favorite book series and she's read it a million times. She's also seen the movies a million times. I wonder if it's close enough for us to make a little detour and visit the home of the fictional vampires she loves so much...

I pull out my phone from my pocket and stealthily Google search. Unfortunately, Forks is a four and a half hour drive from where we're staying this weekend. Dang. We're only staying one night before the races and the leaving the next morning after so there isn't enough time to rent a car and drive out there. But I make a mental note to remember Forks. Maybe I can surprise Keanna on our next anniversary with a trip to see her favorite book's location.

"What are you grinning about?" Keanna says, playfully nudging me with her knee.

I slip my phone back into my pocket. "Nothing."

BREE AND AVERY are here in Washington for the races. Unfortunately, Aiden's girlfriend Jenn couldn't make it this week. But at least Keanna has two of her friends here, so I don't feel as guilty when I have to abandon her to go do Team Loco things before the races. The girls decided to hang out in our hotel room today instead of hanging out at the track for the meet-and-greet. They didn't specifically say the reason why, although I feel like it's pretty obvious. They can have more fun hanging out together away from the fangirls.

They'll show up at the track later to watch us race. If I'm being honest, all the stuff that happens before the race can get old really quickly. Sometimes I don't even want to be here all day. I just want to race. And I'm positively itching to race today after being forced to stay home for the last three races in a row. I'm desperate to get back out on the track, on my bike, doing what I love. Every muscle in my body is aching to ride.

Luckily, there's no more fans accosting me during today's meet-and-greet. Everyone is polite and lovely and I sign a bunch of autographs and have a good time. Once that's over and we get a few laps of practice in, I hydrate and relax with my teammates in our Team Loco trailer. Marcus comes in and gives us the fifteen minute warning, meaning we need to be dressed, on the bikes, and heading to the starting line in fifteen minutes. I turn off my phone and stash it in my locker and then go in search for Keanna. I saw Bree a few minutes ago, so I know the girls have arrived. Where's Keanna?

I step outside of the trailer and look around. She's not hanging out where the bikes are kept like she sometimes does. I don't see her anywhere around. I do see Avery and Clay taking a selfie, so I walk over to them.

"Where's Keanna?"

Avery frowns, glancing around. "She's not with you?"

"No, I haven't seen her."

"That's weird. She was here a few minutes ago."

Okay. I know the odds of Keanna getting kidnapped by a crazy fan are like... very low. Right? But why am I suddenly panicky feeling? I turn around and find Bree, asking her the same question.

"Umm," Bree says, glancing around as if she'll suddenly see Keanna. "She might have gone to the bathroom or something."

"But she's here, right?" I say.

"Yep. We took a taxi here together."

I take a deep breath. "Okay, I'll text her."

She doesn't reply to my text, or my call. The bathrooms are clear across the massive track and I don't have enough time to rush over there and find her. But even as Marcus starts calling for us to get suited up and head to the starting line, I know I won't be able to function if I don't find out that my wife is okay. It's not like her to just leave her friends and not even come say hi to me before a race. Something had to have happened. And the more I think about it, the more terrified I become.

NINE

KEANNA

Jett: Babe? Where are you? You're okay, right?

Jett: Please reply. I'm freaking out here.

I STARE AT THE TEXTS, my phone shaking in my hand as I lean against the wall of a public bathroom stall. Not two minutes after we got here did I suddenly get sick again. It's been weeks since I've felt bad and I thought I was over this. I'm not even that nervous right now. The idea of being around Jett while he did another meet-and-greet had given me so much anxiety that we just stayed at the hotel. I thought that was enough to make me feel better. Apparently not.

My stomach tightens and a shudder of nausea ripples through me. I hate this feeling. It's so awful. I wouldn't even wish it on my worst enemy, not even on all the fangirls who absolutely hate me. With my phone in my hand, I type as fast as my shaking fingers will allow me because I hate knowing Jett is freaking out. I need to reassure him.

Me: I'm fine, sorry. Bathroom! Be there soon.

But it won't be that soon, because I'm starting to feel like I'm going to puke again.

Jett: they're making us line up for the races...
I'll probably miss you.
Me: Sorry, babe. I love you! Good luck!
I'll be watching. :)

He replies something but I don't read it because I have to throw up again. Dry heaving comes in waves.

As soon as I start to feel better, I'm suddenly sick again. I don't know how long passes. Maybe another fifteen minutes.

"Are you okay?" a feminine voice says from the other side of the bathroom stall.

"Yeah," I say, feeling heat rush to my cheeks. "Just a little nauseous."

"Need me to go get help?" she asks.

"No, I'm fine."

Finally, when my throat is sore and I'm positively sick of being in a public bathroom, I open the stall door and step out. The girl who had talked to me is still here, looking worried in the mirror reflection as she washes her hands in the sink. She's probably about my age, with dark hair in two low braids and a hot pink motocross baseball cap on her head.

"You sure you're okay?"

I start to tell her that I'm perfectly fine, but then I heave a sigh. I'm too tired to assure some stranger that I'm perfectly fine. "I think I just had too much coffee and not enough food this morning," I say, plastering on a crooked smile. "I'll be okay."

She dries her hands on a paper towel and tosses it in the trash. "Are you sure?"

I nod. We walk out of the restroom together and back out into the bright summer sun. The rumble of dirt bikes fill the air along with the booming voice of the track announcer that blasts out of every speaker overhead. It's a fairly long walk from these restrooms all the way to the main track where Jett is racing. They take twenty laps, so it's a good thirty minutes for the race. I have time to get there and see the second half of the race, so long as I hurry.

But as I walk quicker, my stomach feels more uneasy. I slow down, grimacing as I pass a taco truck. The smell of food makes my stomach hurt, which so not fair because I freaking love taco trucks. I walk by a cotton candy vendor and even the scent of sugar makes me feel sick. What the heck is wrong with me.

I stop walking, bracing myself on a wooden light pole for a few seconds while I gather my breath and close my eyes, willing the nausea to go away.

"You really don't look okay."

That same girl from the restroom is here now, probably having followed me for the last few minutes.

"I'll be fine. I just need to sit down."

"Well, let's sit," she says, motioning toward a bench a few feet away.

I shake my head. "No, I need to see the race."

I don't say why. Even though I'm sick, I know better than to reveal who I am. This girl clearly doesn't recognize me as Jett Adams' wife, because if she did, she'd probably be laughing at my illness or spewing hateful words about how I stole Jett from the rest of the world. I need to make sure I keep it that way. She can't know who I am, and she can't know that I'm here to watch Jett.

I smile. "Well, I guess I don't *need* to see the race, I just wanted to see it."

"You can watch it on TV," she says, motioning for me to follow her. "Come on. I'll get you some water."

I don't know why I follow this total stranger. Maybe I am dehydrated and delirious from feeling so sick. She walks me just a few feet away to a motorhome that's parked behind a T-shirt stand. It's a nice motor home, probably close to a million dollars if I had to guess. It's like something a famous band would use to tour across the country. The cold air conditioning feels great as I walk inside, and sure enough, there's a large flat screen TV in the kitchen area of the motorhome that's playing the current race. The races are aired live on TV, but they have a three minute delay.

"Let's get you some water," she says, opening a fridge and handing me a bottled water. "You should sit down."

I drop into a leather armchair and slowly sip on the water while I watch the race on the TV. Jett is in third place. He soars over a jump and then takes a sharp left turn as the track winds around. Someone else passes him, putting him in fourth place. Dammit! I clench my teeth so I don't show any emotion about Jett getting further behind.

"My dad runs the merch tables at every professional race, so I've seen most of the races through this television even though I'm physically at each one," she says with a snort. "If I go outside, he makes me help him sell T-shirts, and I hate selling T-shirts. But I dropped out of college because I hate college, and my dad's all 'blah, blah, if you're not in school, you're here with me working'..." She sticks out her tongue. "He's so annoying."

I just smile at her, because I don't have much to say. I loved college, even though it was hard. Of course, I'm really nervous now, because if she goes to every motocross race, she probably knows the professional racers by name. Which means she'd probably recognize my name. I need to stay quiet and make sure I don't accidentally reveal myself to her.

"I'm Caroline, by the way." Caroline gets a water bottle for herself and sits across from me in another armchair.

This motorhome is so nice, it's better than the hotel we're staying at in town. I take a long sip of my water to avoid replying to her. If this were any other situation, I'd tell her my name. A proper, friendly introduction. But Keanna isn't exactly a super common name, and in the motocross world, it's even more rare. I don't want to say my name out loud.

I keep sipping the water and watching the race. Jett isn't doing any better after a few more laps. He's still in fourth place, but the TV is a few minutes behind. Maybe he's caught up to first place by now. My nerves are on overdrive as I watch, anxiously hoping to see him succeed.

"You're looking a little better," Caroline says. "How do you feel?"

"Better," I say with a nod. "I don't feel like puking right now, so that's an improvement."

She smiles, her head tilting slightly as she looks at me. "Maybe you ate something bad."

I shrug. "I haven't eaten much of anything, actually. It's been happening a lot but I don't know why I'm always sick for no reason."

Her eyebrows shoot up high into her forehead. "It's been happening a lot?"

"Yeah, it's annoying."

She leans forward in her chair. "Any other symptoms?"

I consider it, then shake my head. "Not really. I mean, I'm hungry all the time but that's probably because I go through these bouts of puking, so my stomach is empty."

Her bottom lip curls under her teeth. I glance back at the TV, but the camera is focusing on the first and second place racers, not Jett, who might be even further back now. I get the weird feeling I'm being watched, so I look down and sure enough, Caroline is still staring at me with the weirdest look on her face.

"What?" I say, suddenly feeling very awkward. "I'm sorry, I feel better now, so I should get going."

"No, you're fine," she says, holding out a hand to stop me when I try to get up. "You can stay as long as you need."

"Okay, but you're looking at me weird. I didn't mean to intrude or anything." I realize now that someone with a motorhome this nice is probably way too rich to care about random strangers. Maybe she has no idea about any of the professional racers or their wives, because it seems like she's only here at the races because her dad makes her. I finish my bottle of water and twist the cap back on. "I should get going."

"Okay, but..." She bites her lip. "Look, it's probably none of my business or anything, but... your symptoms? They're kind of classic symptoms."

"What do you mean?" I ask, fears that I might have some horrible disease racing through my mind. After my mom's cancer treatment a couple of years ago, I don't want to even think about another sickness in the family.

Caroline scrunches up her nose and then smiles. "Sounds like you're pregnant."

TEN

JETT

DESPITE HAVING STARTED hundreds of races all by myself without Keanna to kiss me good luck, I'm having a hard time dealing with this time. I've literally been racing since before I ever met her. I've ridden my bike to the starting line more times than I can count, waited for the gate to drop, and took off a million times. All by myself. And now, this one time she's not here before the race starts, it's like I'm falling apart. She finally replied to my text so I know she's safe and not kidnapped or anything, but I hate knowing that she's feeling sick again. The whole race almost feels jinxed without her here to tell me good luck.

I can't concentrate. I'm in the middle of the pack before I even know it, and I've almost forgotten how to race like this. I'm not used to being surrounded by other racers. I'm used to leading the pack, sometimes battling it out for the first or second spot. Right now, I'm so far back from first place I'm not even sure where I am on the scoreboard.

Anxiety builds up as I slip further back. I can't lose this race. It's my first race back after being suspended for three races, and people will think something bad is going on if I totally screw up this week. I'm supposed to come back with a fury, soaring through the sky and swallowing up the competition, reminding the corporate big wigs at Team Loco why they want Jett Adams on their team.

Instead, I'm flailing.

My heart races and my hands feel sore as they grip the handlebars. I take a deep breath, lean forward on my bike, the balls of my feet planted solidly on the foot pegs, and concentrate on the bike in front of me. It's a Honda with some number I don't recognize. That's not good—it means this is some newbie racer who isn't popular enough for me to know him by name.

Newbie racers are at the back of the pack. Not cool.

I pin the throttle and fly past him, gaining one spot closer to the front. As we cross the finish line, I glance up at the digital sign and see that we're halfway through the race. That's not great, but it's better than being near the end. I speed up, riding hard and a little bit sloppy, trying to catch up with the next bike.

I recognize the next racer, at least. It's Charlie Baker from Team Yamaha. He's never had a podium finish. I catch up to him on a tabletop jump and pass him quickly. Thoughts of Keanna keep pushing into my mind, but I try to push them right back out and focus. I am worried about her, but deep down I know she'd want me to concentrate on the race, not worry needlessly about her. There are only a few laps left. I'll be done and back with my wife in no time.

When the digital sign has counted down to one remaining lap, I give it my all, but it's still not good enough. When I cross the finish line, I see at least two bikes in front of me. I'm focusing so hard on my own riding that I don't even notice of those two bikes are from Team Loco, or somewhere else. All I know is it's done.

I didn't win.

But the race is over.

I sit up straight on my bike as I ride slowly off the track and down the long dirt corridor that takes me back to where the Team Loco truck is parked. You're not supposed to go out of first gear when riding back here, so it's a long, painfully slow trip.

Finally, I'm back. My mechanic takes the bike from me as I slip off it and toss my helmet on a nearby folding chair. Sweat streams down my face. My teammates are pulling off their boots and changing clothes like we normally do, but I walk straight toward the trailer, needing to see Keanna.

She's not there.

Bree is making Zach a sandwich at the kitchenette. I ask her if she's seen Keanna.

"Um, not in a while, actually. She's not with you?"

I don't even answer. I'm too worried to talk pointless chit-chat when I don't know where my freaking wife is. I jog out of the trailer and head toward the public restrooms, which are located in a building way across the motocross park.

It's a stupid move. I should have had someone from the mechanic team go find her, but I don't want to wait that long. Also I forgot my phone back in my bunk on the Team Loco trailer, so now I'm power-walking in full riding gear across a big facility filled with fans. I flat out ignore a few people who yell my name, and when someone asks for an autograph I say, "Give me a minute," and then just keep walking.

Most people see the look on my face and ignore me though, which is good. They probably think I'm angry about whatever place I finished in the race, but I couldn't care less about that right now.

I need Keanna.

Finally, I arrive at the bathrooms. The women's door is to the right. I shuffle back and forth on my feet for a few seconds until a woman finally walks by.

"Hey!" I say, running up to her and scaring the crap out of her by the looks of it. "Sorry to bother you, but can you see if my wife is in there?"

"Sure," the woman says. She looks older than my mom, but she must be a fan because she pushes open the bathroom door and yells, "Keanna? Are you in here?"

Sometimes it's still so weird to me that total strangers know my name and my wife's name. Some people even know these obscure personal details about us because they heard me answer some random question in an interview one time and they never forgot it.

The woman slips into the bathroom and emerges a few seconds later.

"I checked every stall," she says. "No one's in there."

"Thank you." I give her a smile so she doesn't go

start rumors that Jett and Keanna are breaking up or something and that I don't know where my wife is. Then I decide to lie a little bit just to make sure no rumors start. "My phone is dead so I can't get ahold of her." I chuckle like it's no big deal.

"Sorry, honey," she says, patting me on the shoulder as she walks by. "Hope you find her soon."

"Me too," I mutter as I look around frantically. "Me too."

ELEVEN
KEANNA

"NO WAY." I shake my head. "There's no way."

But even as the words leave my mouth, I'm thinking the opposite. Because there is a way, of course. there is a way I'm pregnant. I just... can't believe it.

"Have you had any other symptoms?" Caroline asks.

"I'm hungry all the time, except for when I'm nauseous," I say as I mull it over. "And my boobs hurt all the time."

Caroline smiles. "Girl... you're probably pregnant."

My head snaps up and I meet her eyes. I'm not exactly scared. And I'm not panicking. I'm just... I draw in a deep breath and cover my hands over my face. "Oh my gosh. Oh my gosh."

When I look up again, Caroline is still sitting next to me, grinning in this happy way. Not a sinister way. Which is good news, I guess.

"Jett is going to be so excited!" she says, clapping her hands together.

My blood runs cold. "What did you just say?"

"That Jett is going to be excited!" She bounces up and down in her chair a bit, then glances up at the TV. The races are over, and the TV announcers are talking to the winner on the podium. The winner is not Jett, but I can't even think about that right now. Who cares if he didn't win a race? I might be having a baby.

Caroline leans over and playfully smacks my knee. "You should go tell him!"

"You know who I am?" I say, feeling a flood of emotions pour over me. This whole time she knew my identity and could have like, I don't know—held me hostage or something. But she didn't. So, while I'm glad she's not a psycho, she still knows this very, *very*, important detail of my personal life.

She rolls her eyes. "I've been working the merch table at races my whole life. Of course I know who you are."

"But... you didn't say anything. You helped me out and you haven't said anything until now."

Her brows furrow. "...Yes? I'm sorry. I didn't know it was a big deal."

I shake my head and lean back in my chair, hoping I'll stop feeling panicky and dizzy soon. "I'm just not used to motocross fans being nice to me. Most of them, women especially, hate me."

"Oh," she says softly as recognition dawns on her face. "Oh, right. You do get a lot of hate on social media, huh?"

I snort a laugh in response. "Depends on your definition of *a lot*."

"Aww, I'm sorry. That's really crappy and you don't deserve it at all."

"Thanks." I smile politely hoping we can change the subject soon. With everything going on right now, the last thing I need is to be reminded of how awful people can be.

"Are you feeling better?" she asks.

"For the most part."

"Well, you should go find your husband and tell him the good news."

I bite my lip. "I don't know for sure that I'm... you know..." I draw in a nervous breath. "I can't even say it out loud right now. I guess I'm in shock."

"Come on," she says, standing up and motioning for me to follow her. "Let's get you back to Jett."

The good news is that my stomach feels much better as I walk out of the motorhome and back into the sunny summer day. The bad news is that my emotions are all over the place. I want to tell Jett, but I'm scared to tell Jett. I don't even know anything for sure. I'll need a pregnancy test as soon as possible, and it's not like they sell those in the concession stand here. Maybe I shouldn't tell Jett anything until I know for sure.

As Caroline and I reach the Team Loco trailer, I turn to her, a pleading look on my face. "Do you think you could please not tell anyone?"

"I won't tell a soul," she says, giving me a smile that looks truly sincere.

I'm still a little nervous because I've learned that you can't really trust anyone when it comes to people's incurable need to gossip online. But I want to trust Caroline. She's been so kind to me and she never once acted like a gossipy fan.

"Thank you," I say. I give her a quick hug.

"I'm at all these events, so you come find me if you ever need anything." She waves as she starts walking away. "Just look for the T-shirt booth!"

I wave goodbye and then turn back toward the

Team Loco trailer. Fans mill about, and I see Aiden signing a baseball cap for a small child. I don't immediately see Jett, so I walk toward the trailer, hoping he's in there changing clothes or something.

"Hey, Keanna, Jett is looking for you," Bree calls out, waving at me with one hand. The other hand is holding a tray of nachos.

"Do you know where he is?" I ask.

"I'm here." Jett appears on the other side of me, face dripping with sweat. He's slightly out of breath as if he'd been running, but he did just finish a race a few minutes ago, so that's probably why. He's still dressed in his full racing gear, minus the helmet. I glance around and notice every other Team Loco racer is wearing shorts and T-shirts.

Jett crushes me into a hug. "I lost you."

"No, you didn't," I say with a little laugh. Funny, how being incased in Jett's arms temporarily makes me forget all about every stress and worry I've ever had. But when he releases me and I take a step backward, all my worries crash back into me.

I don't know how to tell him.

Or if I even should tell him right now.

TWELVE
JETT

I DON'T WANT to let Keanna out of my sight. She assures me she's totally fine and that she had just felt a little sick and went to the bathroom, but I can't help myself. I don't want anything to happen to her. I never want to be away from her ever again. But she makes me let go of her hand after a few minutes when she tells me to change clothes because I stink.

There's a small bathroom in the Team Loco trailer, but it doesn't have a shower. We usually head to the hotel room as soon as possible after a motocross race so we can shower. The supercross races, which are held in stadiums around the country, usually have locker rooms and showers on sight, but not out here in the wilderness of motocross tracks.

I change out of my riding gear and spray air freshener all over the place. As long as you're not too close to me, I don't think I smell bad, but Keanna is sitting in a fold out chair next to the other girlfriends, still looking upset. I don't think she's upset about me, though. She's never really cared if I smell like sweat after a race.

I'm not about to ask her what's wrong in front of all our friends. It's not like she'd tell me, and I'd only draw attention to how weird she's acting. When everyone starts talking about where we all want to go out to dinner tonight, I use the opportunity to sneak Keanna away from the group for a few minutes.

"You want to ditch them and order takeout at our hotel with me?" I ask.

She nods, looking almost grateful for the suggestion. "That would be good."

<hr/>

ONCE WE'RE BACK at our hotel, Keanna is still acting weird. But I'm not quite sure what kind of weird. She's not mad at me. I know how she acts when she's mad at me, and this isn't it. She's reserved, and quiet. Contemplative.

I take a quick shower before I try to figure out

what's wrong with her. When I emerge, dressed in a fresh pair of clothes and smelling nice, I find her laying on the bed watching the hotel TV.

"Babe, what's going on?"

"Nothing," she says with a yawn. "I'm tired."

"Is that all that's wrong with you?" I walk over, sitting on the edge of the bed, my hand reaching out and touching her leg. "You seem upset about something. Are you still feeling sick?"

"Not really," she says. She slowly sits up, crossing her legs and letting her hands hang limply in her lap.

"Key... you're scaring me. What's wrong?"

She bites her lip so hard I expect to see blood pour out of it any second now. When her eyes slowly meet mine, the look she gives me scares the crap out of me. Whatever it is, this is serious.

"Baby?" I ask, sick with worry, and fearful for whatever she's going to say. Is she about to leave me? Confess her love for someone else? My heart races.

"I..." she says, teeth digging into her bottom lip again as she looks down at her lap and then back up at me. "I wasn't going to tell you yet, because I don't know any details yet. It might be nothing."

"Did someone start another rumor online about us?" I ask.

She shakes her head.

"So what is it?"

She takes a deep breath which puffs out her chest. I feel like her lungs are going to expand forever, but then she finally stops, slowly exhales, and says, "I might be pregnant."

I burst into a grin. "Seriously?"

She shrugs. "I don't know! I don't know... I really don't."

My heart floods with warmth and I'm so giddy I want to laugh, but it feels wrong to laugh right now so I try my best to hold it together. "If you don't know for sure, then what makes you think you're pregnant?"

"I have a few weird symptoms," she says, her lips sliding to the side of her mouth. "Namely, the throwing up... you know morning sickness doesn't always happen in the morning? Apparently, that's a myth. It can happen anytime."

I take both of her hands in mine. "Okay, well let's find out. Let's get a test. There's got to be a drug store around here somewhere, let's go buy one."

Her eyes widen. "Are you kidding? All the Team Loco fangirls have been hanging out in the lobby for hours, just dying to catch a glimpse of you guys. If you leave, they'll follow you and see what we're buying, and then our news will be all over the internet."

"That's... a good point," I say, frowning. "Damn. I don't want to wait until we get home. I want to know now."

"Me too," she says, heaving a sigh.

"Wait... are you not happy about this?" I ask her, squeezing her hands.

"I don't know." She says it so simply, so straightforward. "It wasn't really in the plan."

"Sure, it was." We talk about our future kids all the time.

"The plan was to get a puppy," she says with a snort. "Not a kid. Not now, at least."

I lean forward and kiss her. "What about both?"

"A puppy and a kid? Are you crazy?"

"Crazy in love with you," I say, wrapping her in my arms.

She sighs sarcastically, but she's smiling as she leans against me, relaxing all her stress and worries into my arms. We sit here for a moment, caught up in each other's love and the warmth and happiness that comes with being together, alone, quiet, and peaceful.

But I am really dying to find out if I'm about to be a dad.

"Babe?" I whisper as we cuddle on the freshly-made hotel sheets. "I have an idea..."

She peers up at me with a coy smile. "I'm listening."

Half an hour later, there's a knock at our hotel door. I leap up and run over to it, having already waited what feels like a lifetime for this moment. Marcus stands on the other side of the door with a giant paper bag of food with a restaurant logo on the side.

"Umm..." I say, peering at him quizzically. "I didn't ask for food."

"No, dummy, but I'm smarter than you," he says, walking inside the hotel room and quickly closing the door behind him. He sets the bag on the table and pulls out a drugstore bag from inside, holding it up triumphally. "I hid the real goods inside the food. Can't have fans seeing this bag in my hands and wondering what it's for, now can we?" He's grinning his stupid cheesy grin as I snatch the bag from his hands.

Marcus chuckles then starts walking toward the door. "The food is for you guys since you skipped out on dinner with us tonight. Miss Key?" he says, peering over my shoulder to look at Keanna. "Good luck."

"Thanks," she says with a bashful smile.

Marcus fist bumps my shoulder. "Can't wait to find out if we're having a future member of Team Loco."

I roll my eyes as I walk him to the door. "Thanks, man."

Once he's gone, I whirl around to find Keanna sitting on the bed, the ripped open pregnancy test box in front of her. She reads all the instructions out loud, but it's pretty easy to figure out what to do. She's been drinking water ever since we sent Marcus on our secret errand, and now it's all about to pay off.

I follow her to the bathroom and she tops, holds out a hand, and places it on my chest. "What are you doing?"

"Um... taking the test?"

She quirks an eyebrow. "You know I have to pee on the stick, not you?"

"Of course."

"So you can't come in with me!"

I poke out my bottom lip. "But I want to."

"Ew, no!" she says, giggling. "I'm not going to pee in front of you. Gross. You wait out there."

And then the door slams in my face. I chuckle to myself. Drag my hand through my hair. Pace the small hotel room. It probably only takes her a few seconds, but it feels like hours. Finally the door opens and Keanna emerges looking white as a ghost while holding the little plastic pregnancy test.

I'm so eager to find out the results that I can't speak. All I can do is stand here, mouth slightly open, eyes wide, desperate to know our future.

She tips the stick toward me.

"It's positive."

THIRTEEN
KEANNA

YOU'D THINK Jett just won the lottery with how he's acting. I've never seen him smile so big. Never seen him act so weightless, just floating around the room in an excited reverence, as if he'd just been declared the World's Best Motocross Racer, and won every award on the planet, and also been crowned King of the Universe.

But in truth, he's not any of that. He's just a guy, and I'm just a woman, and we're about to have a kid.

A kid!

A real, living, human being. One who will rely on us for every single thing for years until they grow up and can take care of themselves. A tiny little human is growing inside of me right now. I didn't even realize it myself—a stranger figured it out before

I did. I guess I've been so stressed with graduating school and traveling with Jett and avoiding obsessed fangirls that I never even noticed that I've missed two periods.

And if I couldn't be responsible enough to figure that out, how am I supposed to raise a child?

"I'm so happy, I'm starving," Jett says as he dives into the food Marcus had left us. "Is that a thing? Does extreme happiness just make your body burn up all your food and you need more fuel to keep going?"

He doesn't wait for my answer, he just dives back into the bag and gets another taco.

"Babe, you want to eat something?" he says over a mouth full of food. He wiggles his eyebrows. "You're eating for two now."

I touch my stomach. It's too soon to feel anything there, but I've got the most expensive brand of pregnancy test they make sitting right here on the nightstand that tells me there is something in my uterus. Just below my hand.

"I'm not really hungry," I say.

"You should try to eat something," Jett urges. "If you get hungry later, the hotel room service food totally sucks."

I heave a sigh and join him at the hotel room's

tiny table. He's right. The food in the hotel restaurant isn't good at all, and the smell of the takeout does smell pretty delicious. I get a taco and some chips and salsa. Marcus knows us well. The bag is filled with tacos.

"I'm so excited," Jett says as he eats like a horse. "I'm going to be a dad. And you'll be a mom."

"That is how that works," I say sarcastically.

"Babe," Jett says, swallowing his food. "I'm still in shock. I can't believe it. Do you know how far along you are?"

I touch my stomach again and shake my head. "No clue. A couple of months, maybe?"

His eyes widen. "Really?"

I shrug.

"This means I'll be a dad in seven months instead of nine." He counts on his fingers. "Our baby will be born sometime in February? Maybe even on Valentine's day!"

I chew a bite of food and let him continue to talk, hypothesizing all about our child's birth date, gender, hair, and eye color. I try to smile since he's so happy, but I'm still just so weirded out about it. I'm not even sure why. Of course Jett can be happy about this... his body isn't growing a child inside of it. He doesn't have to stress like I do.

"Who are we calling first?" Jett says after finishing his fourth taco. "My parents or your parents? Or just get them all together on speakerphone... that's a better idea."

He checks the time on his phone. "It's already nine o'clock in Texas but they'll all still be awake. Want to call now?"

"No, babe," I say softly, trying not to roll my eyes. "We can't tell them tonight."

"You want it to be in person," he says with a nod. "You're right. It'll be more special that way, but now we have to wait until tomorrow."

"I don't want to tell them tomorrow. It's too early."

He frowns. "Why is it too early?"

"Well, for starters we took a simple drugstore pregnancy test, so we don't know if it's accurate. Maybe it's a false positive."

Jett's face falls. "That can happen?"

I'm not entirely sure, but I do know a girl from one of my old schools who took a test that said she wasn't pregnant, but she really was. If it can display a false negative, maybe it can also display a false positive.

"I need to see my doctor and get confirmation that it's true before we go tell anyone."

Jett's forlorn expression almost makes me feel sorry for him. But then I remember that his body doesn't have to grow a human inside of it and I decide I don't feel sorry for him after all. He reaches across the table and takes my hand. His eyes seem to sparkle beneath the glow of the dim hotel lamp and the television.

"We'll make a doctor appointment first thing tomorrow."

I nod. "That sounds good."

"Babe?" He squeezes my hand.

"Yes?"

"I'm really excited."

I can't help but smile. Not because I agree with him, but because he's so happy it would be impossible to keep this grin off my face.

FOURTEEN

JETT

WE GET the confirmation two days later at our local doctor's office. Even with the blood test results, which the doctor describes as being much more accurate than a urine test, Keanna still doesn't want to tell our family just yet. I agree to support her wishes, but it's killing me inside to keep it all a secret. I want to tell everyone. I want to start decorating the spare room in our house for a baby. I want to make some upgrades to the childcare room at The Track so our baby will have the best care possible while Keanna and I are working. But all I can do is go about my day as if everything is perfectly normal.

The next motocross race is in a week and a half and I'm strongly thinking about canceling the rest of the season. I haven't told Keanna yet because she'll probably freak out and insist that I keep racing. But the truth is, I'd rather be here with her for every moment of the pregnancy. Plus, I've already missed three races this season, so it's not like Team Loco is expecting much of me. I should call this whole season off and just stay home with my wife. But the thought of telling her right now makes me nervous, so now I'm keeping two secrets. The first, is the secret of our baby from everyone else, and the second is this secret from my wife. Ugh. I'm not a fan of secrets.

We do a lot of research and read a ton of reviews before finally choosing the best ob-gyn in this part of Texas. Dr. Lucia Marks has twenty years of experience and is highly respected in her field. Plus, she delivers at the best hospital in the area. I want only the absolute best for Keanna and my unborn child. We have to wait two weeks for an appointment, and Keanna makes me keep our baby a secret the whole time.

Finally, the day of our first appointment is here. Keanna's knee bounces in the truck as I drive to our appointment. "You okay?" I ask her.

"Yep."

"Why do you look so nervous?"

"Because it's awkward," she says, curling her lip.

"They're about to be all up in my business." She waves her hands around her midsection. "It's embarrassing."

"If it'll make you feel better, I'll get naked too."

She bursts out laughing. "They'd probably kick you out for that."

I grin. "Well, I'll help any way I can."

The doctor's office is about twenty minutes away, in a newer, nicer part of town. The building itself is made of glass exterior windows, with expertly manicured tropical plants in the landscaping. It almost feels like going to a resort instead of a doctor. Keanna and I hold hands as we walk inside. The lobby is gorgeous and looks so clean you could probably eat off every surface

We check in and then take a seat in the expansive waiting room, which has plush leather chairs. It's completely the opposite of the rinky-dink worn-out waiting room at our local family doctor. This place is luxurious, which makes me confident that we chose the right doctor. All this fancy stuff has to mean they take pride in what they do.

Keanna picks up a fashion magazine from the table in front of us and flips through it, her knee still nervously bouncing a bit. I wrap my arm around her shoulders and look around the waiting room. Flat screen televisions on the wall are playing various daytime talk shows. Pregnant women are everywhere, some with massive bellies that are probably due any moment, and others barely showing. It's mostly all women here, but I do see a couple of men sitting next to women. They look nervous and bored.

I couldn't be any further from nervous and bored. I'm excited and eager. The only bad part is we'll have to wait several more months until our baby is here. The anticipation will drive me crazy.

We don't have to wait very long and soon we're taken back to see the doctor. First, Keanna gets an ultrasound. I sit next to her in the dimly lit room, holding her hand eagerly as the technician presses the ultrasound wand to her stomach. And then, right there on the screen in black and white, is our baby.

"You're at ten weeks," the technician says, clicking print on the machine. A little copy of the ultrasound prints out and she hands it to Keanna. "This puts your due date right around January thirteenth."

"Awesome," I say.

Keanna looks up at me. There's delight and anxiety in her eyes. She bites her lip. "I guess this is real."

I lean over and kiss her head. We're taken back to

the exam room and then the doctor comes in and does her exam. Then over the next half an hour, we're told so much information about pregnancy that I start to lose track of it all. But the doctor puts Keanna at ease, which makes me happy. Before we leave, we're given a welcome kit that has a diaper bag with the doctor's logo on it, as well as a ton of other baby stuff and lots of coupons and some pregnancy magazines.

Before I know it, we're walking back out to the car. Keanna exhales a long, slow sigh. "That went well."

"I think so, too," I say, opening the passenger door for her. She climbs into my truck then turns to look at me. "January thirteenth."

"January thirteenth," I say back. "We'll be parents."

"Parents," she says.

"Does this mean we can finally tell our family?"

She frowns, sliding her lips to the side of her mouth as she thinks it over. "I suppose so."

"Yay!" I grab her face and kiss her. "I can't wait."

FIFTEEN
KEANNA

EVERYTHING IS HAPPENING TOO QUICKLY. Now that we've got actual ultrasound pictures of our little unborn baby, I can't really keep it a secret anymore. We're going to tell the family tonight over dinner at our house. I've been dreading this moment ever since I took that first pregnancy test in the hotel room. It's not that I'm worried about our family's reactions, it's that I'm worried about myself. Once we tell people, everything changes. I can't keep it to myself anymore. Everyone will know.

And they'll end up thinking the same thing I am.

They'll wonder if I have what it takes to be a good mother.

I was raised by a terrible mother. And although my adoptive mom, Becca, is an amazing human being and nurturing parent, it's not the same. I've only known Becca since I was practically an adult myself. When it comes to babies and toddlers and children—I've only ever known disfunction and chaos. Anger and yelling and getting smacked across the face when I did something wrong as a kid. I wasn't read bedtime stories or taken trick-or-treating, except for a few times my birth mother Dawn was dating some guy with kids of his own and I got to tag along.

My childhood was far from perfect. And now I'm going to raise a kid on my own? I have no idea what I'm doing. The very thought of being a mother has made me more nauseated than the morning sickness. I'm terrified.

Over the past few years, I've watched Becca and Bayleigh raise their children, and I've even helped out. But it's not the same. Sure, I fed and bathed my little brother Elijah when my mom was going through breast cancer treatments, but that was easy. I was like a babysitter. The real mothering still came from our mom, who held Elijah as he slept each night. She's a great mom. Bayleigh is a great mom.

I have no idea what I'm doing.

I might know how to change a diaper, but I don't know about doctor visits and filling out birth certificates and how to take care of a sick baby. I don't know how to teach them to walk or talk or how to be a good person. When I was a little kid I would steal candy from the store because Dawn encouraged it and thought it was funny. It wasn't until I was much older and got caught stealing from my second grade teacher when I was told that stealing is wrong. What if all my natural instincts are messed up? What if this baby will be born and I'll ruin him or her by not knowing what I'm doing?

They didn't teach me how to be a mother in college. They taught me business. I'm good at business. I'm not good at anything else.

Tears fill my eyes as I brush my teeth. They threaten to spill over and ruin my mascara as I apply my makeup. Jett invited our parents over for dinner tonight, but then he insisted on taking care of all the dinner arrangements himself, so I've been up in our bedroom taking a soothing bath and trying to prep myself for what's about to happen. The BBQ he's making out on the grill smells amazing. I hope he remembered to take out the good dishes we use for company, and to turn the ice maker on in the freezer so we don't run out.

I want to be out there helping him get things ready, but before I know it, the doorbell rings and my heart speeds up. Our parents are here, and I've only just finished getting dressed. I guess I also suck at time management, which won't be good for being a mom.

With shaking knees, I walk out to the foyer. Jett runs inside from the back porch where he's been grilling, wiping his hands on the apron tied around his neck. "Are they here?" he says, taking off the apron.

"Yep."

"Awesome!" His whole face is lit up in a smile, which is basically how he's been looking ever since the day we found out we're having a baby. I wish I could be as carefree as him. But Jett was raised by incredible parents so I guess he's not worried at all.

Together, we open the front door and let the family in. My parents, Jett's parents, and our little siblings enter the living room. Mom hugs me and hands me a tray of freshly baked chocolate chip cookies.

"This is fun," Bayleigh says as we walk into the dining room which, I'll be honest, Jett has done a fantastic job of setting up. He did remember the good dishes after all.

"We should have dinner parties at your house

more often," Mom says. "All we have to do is show up and eat."

"Hell yeah," Jace says, taking a seat next to Park at the table. "Smells good, too."

I help Jett bring in the food and soon, we're all eating like the big happy family we are. I look around at the table, all six of us, and try to picture where the seventh chair would go. I guess our baby would be in a high chair for a little while. It feels so surreal knowing there will be another member to the Adams/Park family soon.

In just six and a half short months.

I take a deep breath and then add more sugar to my sweet tea. Dinner goes well. Jett and I decided we'd tell the family our news after the meal is over. But now I'm wishing we had told them sooner, because I'm getting more nervous by the second. I'm fairly sure they'll be happy... I mean, our families love kids. And they love us. They'll be happy.

But I'm so worried that they'll give me a look. A look that says *she won't know how to raise this child.* And even though they'll all be completely justified in thinking this, because it's true, I know I'll be crushed. I love all of these people, and even though I've never truly been good enough to be in their company, they've accepted me anyway. What if this is the final straw that makes them push me away? What if everyone realizes what Jett's fangirls have been saying for years and they decide he'd be better off without me? That he and our baby would be better off without me?

I couldn't survive without this family, without my job at The Track. If they decide I'll be a bad mom and kick me out of the family, I would have nothing.

I sit a little straighter, telling myself not to cry.

Before I know it, Jett squeezes my leg from under the table. When I look over at him, he's giving me the look that means he's ready. His eyes widen just a tad. *You ready?* They seem to say.

I give him a slight nod. I can't hide the pregnancy forever, so it might as well come out now.

"Guess what?" Jett says over the chatter of our family talking.

Everyone looks over at him. He's grinning. I thought he was going to tap his glass with a butterknife and make some big speech or something, but instead he just grins wide and says, "We're having a baby."

My jaw drops. He just said it. Just like that.

Happy chaos ensues over the next few minutes. My mom jumps out of her chair and swallows Jett and me in a huge bear hug. Then Bayleigh does the same. The dads are excited, and Jace starts making fun of Park, calling him Grandpa. Then Park calls Jace Grandpa right back, because all four of our parents are now going to be grandparents.

Elijah claps his hands and gives me a hug, and Brooke asks if she can hold the baby. We have to explain to them that the baby won't be born for a little while, and I think they understand it for the most part.

The rest of the evening doesn't happen at all the way I had imagined it would. Not a single annoyed glance is directed at me. Not a single snide comment. Everyone is so happy. It's like they've all temporarily forgotten where I came from. I'm sure it'll catch up with them later, and they'll tell me that I'm going to be a terrible mother.

But for now, I soak up all the happy vibes.

SIXTEEN
JETT

WHEN THE SUMMER motocross season ends, I finish in sixth place. In my entire amateur and professional career, I've never finished a season so badly. The irony is that I've spent a lifetime training and practicing and conditioning my body to be skilled enough that I never lose a race, because losing had always been the worst case scenario. And now, here I am, a complete series loser by all definitions of the word, I don't even care. Not even one bit. Not even when my teammates try to soothe me by saying nice things like, *you'll win next year*, and *man, this year was just unlucky*. I am completely unbothered, because I have better, bigger things in my life than this.

I have a family.

AMY SPARLING

So far it's still just Keanna and me, but our baby will be here in four months. Keanna is doing really well and our baby is healthy. We've chosen not to know the gender ahead of time, and it's driving our family and friends crazy. Everyone wants to know—will we have a boy or a girl? And I keep telling them they'll find out after our child is born.

I get so many comments from people who assume I'm hoping for a boy to turn into my own little motocross protégé, but that's not true. I'm excited to be a dad. It feels like my life won't be complete until I am a dad, but that feeling that goes down deep in my soul doesn't have a specific gender attached to it. Boy or girl, I'm going to be so thrilled either way.

Besides, I can still turn a girl into my little motocross protégé.

With as happy as I am, sometimes it feels like Keanna isn't all that happy. Which is weird because we've always talked about wanting to have kids one day. But sometimes when we're together, I just get this subtle vibe that maybe she's not thrilled about it. When I ask her, she brushes me off, says I'm being too worried about nothing. But I know her, and I know something isn't quite right. Until she lets me in and tells me what's going on in her mind, I can't help her.

With the racing season over, I've got a lot of time on my hands, most of which I spend at The Track. I help out with motocross lessons, or bother my mom and Bayleigh in the front office. Sometimes, it's fun, and other times I have to go home and hide out because the fangirls are at The Track in abundance.

Today is a fairly chill day. So far, I haven't seen any fangirls. My mom and Keanna decided that we needed new fall-themed decorations for the front lobby, so they ran to the store, leaving me hanging out with my mother-in-law. Since it's slow, she and I are playing this card game she taught me. She swears it was all the hype when she was younger, back before smartphones took over society.

"Have you decided what your grandmother name will be?" I ask her. She and my mom have been discussing it for weeks, trying to come up with the perfect name to call themselves.

"You know I really think I love Grandma. Just nice and traditional, ya know?"

"Isn't that what my mom wants to be called, too?" I say, lifting an eyebrow.

Becca laughs. "Yeah. We both want to be Grandma. And then Park said I could be Grandma

B, but Bayleigh's name also starts with a B, so that's out."

"You can both be Grandma," I say with a shrug. "You're always together, anyhow so Grandma can just be one unifying word that means both of y'all."

"I like your thought process," she says, high fiving me.

As we settle back into another card game, I start wanting to ask her about Keanna. If she's noticed the same thing I am, that Keanna is acting a little like she's not happy for our baby. But even though she's Keanna's mom, I don't want to bring up something this private with her. After all, if Becca saw a problem, maybe she would have already asked me? Maybe it's all just in my head.

The door opens a little while later and Becca's eyes widen in surprise. "What the hell did you buy?" she says, standing up.

I join her at the front of the lobby, where Keanna and my mom are carrying in an outlandish amount of shopping bags. Some are even as tall as Keanna herself.

"We only bought the things we absolutely needed," my mom says.

"Turns out, we needed a lot of things," Keanna says, grinning.

MY ADVENTURE WITH YOU

It looks like one of those home décor stores threw up in our lobby. Becca joins in on the fun as they take out all their new decorations, pull off the wrapping and the tags, and decide where they should go. I help out by doing what they tell me to do, hanging up garland and assembling a large, glittery pumpkin thing. While we fill our lobby with festive décor, I keep an eye on Keanna, trying to decipher if she's happy or not.

Later, when she's walking to her office in the back hallway, I follow her inside and close the door.

"Why'd you close the door?" she asks curiously as she opens a desk drawer and takes out a tube of lip gloss.

"Are you happy?" I ask.

"Huh?" She applies the lip gloss then smacks her lips. "What do you mean?"

I step forward and put my hand on her small belly. It's round and firm to the touch, growing bigger each week. "Are you happy about our baby? Because lately it seems like you're not. And I just want to know why."

She's quiet for a long moment. And then she looks up at me with tears in her eyes. "It's not that I'm not happy..." She takes a long time to say anything else. When she speaks, her words are raw with emotion. "It's just that..."

"You can talk to me, babe." I rest my forehead on hers. "Please talk to me."

"I think I'll be a bad mom."

I take half a step back. Her words are the last thing I'd expect to hear. "Huh?"

"I was raised by a bad mom. And that's going to make me a bad mom."

"Keanna, that's not true at all."

She shakes her head, tears rolling down her cheeks. "You don't know that."

SEVENTEEN

KEANNA

IT'S FRIDAY NIGHT, which is usually date night if Jett isn't out of town at a race. Today at work when I'd asked him where he wanted to go for dinner, he said he had something else in mind. I didn't question him because Jett loves his little surprises he comes up with. Maybe there's a new food truck in town he wants to go to, or an art festival he plans to take us to. When I get out of the shower, I dress in a simple pair of jeans and a black cardigan because it's a little cool outside in this October weather.

When I walk out of the bathroom and into our master bedroom, a flash of color catches my eye. It's pink and white rose petals on the carpeting, trailing to the door. What the heck?

I follow them. The little flowery path takes me

through the house and to the back door. I open it, and step outside. There's a large inflatable projector screen out here, two lawn chairs around a firepit, and a table behind them with takeout bags of food. Tacos, to be specific. My favorite.

"What is this?" I ask Jett, who is on his laptop which is connected to the projector.

He stands up, walks over and takes my hands. "This is proof that you will be an amazing mom."

A lump forms in my throat. "It's been a week since I told him my fears of not knowing how to be a good mom, and I thought he'd just forgotten about it.

"I don't understand," I say.

"Have a seat, and some tacos, and I'll show you."

We get all set up with outdoor TV trays to hold our food, and then Jett presses play on the computer. A video begins on the screen in front of us. It's a little cheesy, obviously edited together by Jett himself.

And it's the best thing I've ever seen.

He's managed to find hundreds of photos and video clips, probably taking them from everyone's phone and social media. Some clips are recorded by Mom, Dad, Bayleigh, and Jace. Some are from Jett's phone, and some I recognize as things I've posted to my own social media page.

It's the history of me and Elijah and Brooke. Of

my little brother's first steps across the carpet in my parents' house, how he walked from Becca's arms into mine, with Park filming, so excited himself that the video footage is shaky because he couldn't hold still. There's a photo of Jett's little sister Brooke and I last Halloween, when we wore a couples costume together. She was Elsa and I was Anna. There are Christmases and birthdays and scenes at the hospital when Becca was battling breast cancer, Elijah asleep in my arms, and me asleep in the hospital chair next to our mom.

There's Brooke and I covered in finger paints, making goofy faces to the camera. There's a picture I never knew existed from years ago, when our parents had gone on a double date, leaving the toddlers with us. In the picture, I'm passed out on a blanket on the living room floor, Elijah and Brooke asleep in my arms, the TV playing cartoons in the background.

It goes on like this for a whole hour. Pictures and videos and all these memories of the last few years of my life. This is how my life is now, with my new family. When it ends, I turn to Jett with tears in my eyes.

"Baby, you've been a mother-like figure to our siblings for years now. You don't have to worry about our own child. You're going to be an amazing mom."

He squeezes my hand and kisses my cheek. "People always ask why both of our moms had kids so late in life, especially my mom because I was practically grown up when she had Brooke. But I think maybe fate had something to do with it. Maybe it was fate that you would come into our lives when you needed a real family. You got to help raise our siblings from their birth, and I know it's not the same as having our own kid, but I know you'll be a great mother. Because you're a great person. You can do anything you set your mind to."

I get out of my chair and walk over to his, settling down into his lap as I wrap my arms around his neck. "Thank you," I whisper.

His arms are strong and secure as they hold me close. We sit here in this moment, two soul mates and our growing baby, and everything feels exactly like it should be. I might have a past that was painful, but it's not the past that matters anymore.

It's the future. Our future.

EIGHTEEN

JETT

Four months later

I PUSH open the heavy metal door, walking swiftly down the narrow hallway that leads to the hospital waiting room. The air smells like coffee and hand sanitizer, a smell I've grown used to in the last twelve hours of labor. As I reach the waiting room, I see my parents, Keanna's parents, and our siblings all half-asleep in the corner of the room. It's three-fifteen in the morning, but it doesn't feel like that to me.

I feel more awake than I've ever been.

I feel so energized, I might never sleep again.

AMY SPARLING

And according to everyone's parenting advice, I probably won't be getting much sleep for the next year, so that's fine with me.

I clear my throat. Dad wakes up first, shaking my mom who had fallen asleep on his shoulder. Park and Becca perk up. Elijah is already awake, and he tugs on Brooke's arm.

They've been here the whole time. All six of them, choosing to wait in the hospital from the moment we arrived after Keanna's water broke while she was working earlier today. Well, yesterday. My mom and Becca kept me fed and filled with fluids, checking in on us every half hour, but choosing to stay in the waiting room so Keanna wouldn't get overwhelmed. The first few hours of labor were fun. We'd eagerly waited and counted down the minutes between contractions until they got closer together and became more painful. Then I held Keanna's hand while she did the most incredible thing she's ever done. Give birth to our first child. Before tonight, I'd thought I loved my wife more than it was possible to love anyone.

Turns out, I could still love her even more.

My family sits up, all eager and wide-eyed, waiting desperately for some kind of news after hours and hours of waiting.

"Well?" my dad says, eyes bright with anticipation.

I grin. "It's a girl."

ABOUT THE AUTHOR

Amy Sparling is the bestselling author of books for teens and the teens at heart. She lives on the coast of Texas with her family, her spoiled rotten pets, and a huge pile of books. She graduated with a degree in English and has worked at a bookstore, coffee shop, and a fashion boutique. Her fashion skills aren't the best, but luckily she turned her love of coffee and books into a writing career that means she can work in her pajamas. Her favorite things are coffee, book boyfriends, and Netflix binges.

She's always loved reading books from R. L. Stine's Fear Street series, to The Baby Sitter's Club series by Ann, Martin, and of course, Twilight. She started writing her own books in 2010 and now publishes several books a year. Amy loves getting messages from her readers and responds to every single one! Connect with her on one of the links below.

www.AmySparling.com

facebook.com/authoramysparling
bookbub.com/profile/amy-sparling
goodreads.com/Amy_Sparling

Printed in Great Britain
by Amazon

78461379R00075